AN AFRICAN SAFARI

CAN YOU SPOT THE LEOPARD?

KAREN B. WINNICK

GREENLEAF
BOOK GROUP PRESS

Published by Greenleaf Book Group Press
Austin, Texas
www.gbgpress.com

Distributed by Greenleaf Book Group

For ordering information or special discounts for bulk purchases, please contact Greenleaf Book Group at PO Box 91869, Austin, TX 78709, 512.891.6100.

Design and composition by Greenleaf Book Group
Cover design by Greenleaf Book Group

Publisher's Cataloging-in-Publication data is available.

Print ISBN: 978-1-62634-975-9
eBook ISBN: 978-1-62634-976-6

Part of the Tree Neutral® program, which offsets the number of trees consumed in the production and printing of this book by taking proactive steps, such as planting trees in direct proportion to the number of trees used: www.treeneutral.com

Printed in Canada on acid-free paper.

22 23 24 25 26 27 28 29   10 9 8 7 6 5 4 3 2 1

First Edition

For Sophia, Jacob, Wesley, Myla, Benny, Sara, Teddy, and Max, with love.

Climb inside the jeep—
We'll drive the bumpy road
Spurting pebbles, dust, dirt,
Keeping alert!

Hundreds of flamingos gather at daybreak,
Bending slender necks, wading on thin legs,
Dipping beaks into the lake to scoop krill quickly,
Before jackals awake.

Acacias appear

Bursting with blossoms *until*

The white storks scatter.

She drops into the world wet,

And in a moment struggles to rise on wobbly legs.

The newborn gazelle shakes and quivers.

She totters and her knees buckle.

She starts up again, but her legs splay.

She kicks off,

pushes *harder—up, up* until

She is standing.

Time to take her first steps.

Across the wet grassy plain,
Five ostriches run in a line,
Girls in front, one boy behind.
Not an ostrich out of place,
Ten long legs keeping pace.

Gazelles, zebras, wildebeests graze all day,
Their bodies still as statues,
But their tails sway
Back and forth,
Wagging fast, wagging slow.
The reason why?
Swatting flies!

Her calf stands close between her legs.

Mother elephant sucks up water in her trunk.

She raises it above her head.

Her great faucet sways . . .

WHOOSH! Wet windy sprays!

Mother-daughter showers.

He rolls his boulder body into thick mud,
Sloshing his trunk like wet rope.
He dunks and splashes in the cool wallow—
A euphoric elephant, sunk in soothing slime.

Elephants gather with their kin.
One mother bellows above the din.
Her smallest beneath her legs,
Another by her side,
Her oldest following behind.
She moves them off,
To eat, to drink and escape the sun.

Then, she leads them back in a run.
Ears flapping, chins tucked in,
Aunts, uncles, cousins greet them
With roars, snorts, and rumbles.
Trunks touch, tusks clack—
A celebration of "Welcome Back!"

His foreleg kicks up dust.
He flaps his ears
And shakes his head in angry thrusts.
Bull elephant's trunk furls high,
Loudly trumpeting a warning cry:
"STEER CLEAR!"

She spears a snake, gulps it whole.
There it goes . . .
On a lumpity, bumpity trek
Down inside stork's long neck.

Giraffe leaves her calf
Near acacia trees,
And wanders off
To nibble leaves.
Not far away,
She munches tender tops.

Suddenly she stops,
To listen, watch.
DANGER!
Quickly,
She lopes back
To protect her calf.

A step, then two,
Cheetah stops, she waits.

She moves again.
She sights her prey.

She leaves her cub
Behind a mound
And slowly creeps
Along the ground.

She halts once more.
She hesitates.

Back and forth,
She turns her face,
To eye her cub,
To spot her prey.

She crouches . . . *POUNCE!*

Food today!

Whose furry face is watching
From its hidden grassy seat,
Waiting hungrily
For Mama's meat to eat?

Does a zebra foal know its mother
From the pattern of her stripes?
From the sound of her whinny?
From the smell of her fur?
Or just by staying close to her?

White egrets perch
Atop rhino's back,
Hitching a ride.
His eyes are weak,
So rhino stops
More than he goes.

When he's too slow,
His stowaways know
To flap their wings
And *fly away.*

Topi stands like
a chieftain,
Atop his dirt mound—

Looking over the plains,
Searching grasses to graze,
Watching for danger.

Under his hooves,
Termites bore out
new tunnels.

Wildebeest is a mixed-up puzzle—
A bit of moose around
the muzzle,
Horse legs long and thin,
But body and skin
Like a buffalo.

The closest kin
To this jumbled stew
Is the gnu.
The two are in fact the same.
The only difference,
The name.

Meerkats recline on the dusty earth,
While one watches from atop his berth.
He's protecting the sun-worshipers
Soaking up sunshine,
Their favorite pastime.

Guinea chicks follow their mama hen.
Oh, but where did they go?
Off the path, they wander so.
Into the grass,
Stuck in the brush,
They need to come back!

Mama's in a rush
To get back to the nest.
Her chicks must eat
And she must rest.

Dik-Diks,
Always a pair,
Nibble green leaves,
Stop and stare,
Disappear.

Reappear,
Then retreat
Back into the bush,
Darting in and out,
Playing hide-and-seek.

Mother lions lie side by side
With their cubs, resting on rocks.

Father presides on the top ledge,
Alone on his throne, protecting his pride.

Marabou stork
Struts about on spindly legs.
Atop his thick red wrinkled neck
Sits a great bald head
With deep dark eyes,
Fuzzy peaks, a pointed beak.

His black wings drape,
a thick night cape
Around his hunched,
paunchy shape.
Silly old man!

Spotted hyena cubs
Drink milk from their mother.
She licks their faces, and off they run
To scratch and bite each other.
Mother makes sure she stays alert.
Her young play wild and rough.
One cub could get hurt.

On the grassy plain,
The black rhino sits idle,
A stalled armored truck.

An old, warped barge,
Long and slow,
Gliding in repose.
Skimming the surface,
Seeming to smile—
A contented crocodile.

Galloping by the river,
zebras in flight
Make blurring patterns
of black and white.

Moving in the water,
Their whirled reflections
of light and dark
Spin into—

Motion art.

Wildebeests stampede
Across the plain, a hurricane,
Trampling grass, whirling
dust in the air.

And one small wildebeest
Searches for his mother—
Everywhere.

First, aardvarks build their den.
When their babies grow, they go.
Hyenas move in then.
When *they* go,
Warthogs come to burrow.

When *they* go,
Jackals arrive at this place.
They want more room—

Growing families need space.

Bushback jumps high,
Darts and prances,
Dances and spins.
Her hooves fly.
Anything to keep
Lion from finding
The tall grass where
Her fawn sleeps.

Every day, hippos choose
To loll and soak and sprawl in ooze.

At night, they climb out of the mud
To search for grass with grunts
and thuds.

Next day, they repeat doing
what they choose,
To loll and soak and sprawl
in ooze.

Back to their burrow,
Warthog father, mother, babies
Trot in a line.

LION!

Four tails like flags
Pop *up! up! up! up!*

Back to their burrow,
Warthog father, mother, babies

RUN! RUN! RUN! RUN!

Vervets are everywhere,
Cavorting in trees,
Climbing on branches,
Scooting through leaves,

Swinging by their tails,
Jumping around . . .

But when an eagle hovers,
Not a vervet can be found.

They make the kill,
So lions are first to feast.
They rip apart the meat.
Even before the lions are done,
A cackle of hyenas come.
Hoping *they'll* get to eat,
Jackals come by and wait.
Vultures are last to arrive.
They clean the plate.

All morning,
Baboons *pick pick pick*
Each other's fur.

They *pick pick pick*
To get the parasites,
Before they bite.

All evening,
Baboons *pick pick pick*
Each other's fur.

By day, bat-eared foxes
Conceal themselves from sight.

But their eyes glisten
Like small moons in the night.

High in a tree,
Two lions rest.
Light fades, sun sets.
One suddenly rises
With thunderous *ROARS*.
But the other sleeps
And snores, snores.

Guinea hens
squawk, squawk
Because leopard stalks.

Can you spot the leopard
In a glint of moonlight,
Slipping out to stalk,
Under cover of the night?

Can you spot his pattern
Through the shadow of the trees,
A prowler in the dark,
Stealing past on silent feet?

Can you spot his tail
Above the swaying reeds,
As he hunts his quarry
In a spurt of might and speed?

Can you spot the leopard
In the waning moonlight,
High in the branches, feeding
Under cover of the night?

It's late.
Time to return to camp.
Wash up, eat, and sleep
Under a vast blanket of stars.
Dreaming safari dreams.

AFRICAN SAFARI ANIMALS

AARDVARKS sleep in burrows all day, curled in a ball. At night they climb out to hunt for ants and termites. Their long snouts sense vibrations of insects below the ground. Their sticky tongues lap up as many as fifty thousand termites at one time. While they eat, their oversize ears swivel, scanning for danger. If they detect a predator, they quickly dig a hole and hide.

BABOONS live in troops of about fifty members. Most days they arise early, and while their young play, adults groom each other. Then they set off in their territory to search for food. Evenings they return to their sleeping sites and spend more time grooming.

BAT-EARED FOXES live in small families in underground dens. At night they come out into open grassland to groom, play, and look for food. Their favorite food is termites, which they crunch with their sharp teeth. They have as many as fifty teeth, more than most mammals.

BUSHBUCKS are shy, solitary antelopes that prefer to live close to forests rather than in open land. When a female gives birth, she cleans her newborn and hides it well while she looks for food. When she returns, she nurses her calf and even eats its dung, so there's no smell to attract a predator.

Powerful hunters, **CHEETAHS** are the fastest land animals, with spurts of speed of up to sixty miles an hour. They hunt by day, unlike lions and leopards that hunt at night. Their spots enable them to hide in tall grasses, as they stalk their prey and leap out for the kill.

CROCODILES spend most of their time with their bodies underwater while their eyes, on top of their heads, look around. Even at night, their eyesight, hearing, and sense of smell are excellent. Their teeth are sharp, and their bite is among the strongest of any animal.

DIK-DIKS stay a pair for life. They blend into their surroundings, where bushes provide plenty of cover. They eat leaves and fruits, providing them with enough water so they seldom need to drink. When the female senses danger she makes a whistling noise through her nose, sounding like "dik-dik." They run away fast, zig-zagging between the shrubs.

Cattle **EGRETS** live in dry, grassy fields and feed alongside large grazing animals like rhinos. When the animals move, they kick up grasshoppers, crickets, flies, and earthworms, which the cattle egrets eat. Cattle egrets hitch rides on the animals' backs, bobbing their heads with each step as they peck at ticks.

The largest land animals, African **ELEPHANTS** live in herds of mothers and their young, sisters, and female cousins. Males stay with the herd until they are about fourteen, then join a loose group of bull elephants. Elephants use their long trunks for breathing, smelling, grasping, caressing, sucking up water, and detecting vibrations.

FLAMINGOS' pink color comes from pigments in the small crustaceans they eat. They are very social and sometimes gather in groups of thousands, where they stretch their long necks and move rhythmically from side to side.

Mother **GAZELLES** hide their offspring in tall grasses on the savanna. Newborns curl up and stay hidden from predators for days and even weeks. Their mothers come back to nurse them until they are old enough to join the herd.

The tallest land animals, **GIRAFFES** eat leaves from the tops of acacia trees, which other animals can't reach. Because the leaves contain a lot of water, giraffes can go for a long time without drinking. When they are thirsty, they must bend low to drink and become easy prey for lions.

GUINEA fowl spend their time scratching the ground for insects and worms, seeds, and berries. Hens pick sheltered spots on the ground to build nests of twigs and leaves. The chicks, called keets, follow their mother everywhere until they're big enough to be on their own. Whenever danger threatens, guinea fowl sound an alarm with loud squawks.

To stay cool, **HIPPOS** spend their days in the water. Their nose, eyes, and ears are on top of their head so they can breathe, see, and hear while their huge barrel-shaped bodies remain underwater. If they completely submerge, they're able to hold their breath for a long time. At night, hippos leave the water to feed, mostly on grass.

Spotted **HYENAS** live in clans of up to eighty members. Females are larger and one rules the clan. A mother gives birth and nurses two to four cubs a year in their den. Spotted hyena cubs scuffle with each other for food and ranking.

JACKALS hunt at night, but in more remote places they'll search for food in daylight. They mate for life and are members of larger packs. They communicate with yaps, howls, yips, and growls only with their own family, ignoring other jackals.

LEOPARDS live alone and hunt at night. With great strength and strong climbing ability, they drag their kill up into a tree to hide it from other animals. Often they will leave their kill for days and return when they're hungry. Their spots, called rosettes, help them to blend in and make them difficult to see.

LIONS are the most social big cats, residing in groups called "prides" of ten to fifteen animals, sometimes more. From dusk to dawn they hunt zebras, wildebeests, impalas, and other mammals. While males protect their pride and their territory with roars and scent-markings, lionesses do most of the hunting.

MARABOU storks behave more like vultures than storks. Mostly they feed on dead animal scraps called carrion. They also devour garbage and poop and live small animals such as frogs, fish, birds, and reptiles. Sometimes before they eat, they wash their food in water.

MEERKATS live in large family groups called mobs. Everyone takes part in finding food, caring for the young, and acting as sentries to watch for predators. Sentries perch upright on high rocks or mounds to scan for hawks, eagles, or jackals. If danger is sensed, they let out shrill squeals. The mob scrambles into their burrow.

OSTRICHES are the largest, heaviest birds. They can't fly but run faster than any other bird, up to 43 miles an hour. When they run, their wings help to keep them balanced. Ostriches live in groups of one male and several females. Their long necks and good eyesight help them to see far and avoid danger.

White **RHINOS** are grazers, munching grass on the plains. Black rhinos are browsers, with pointed upper lips that pull off leaves and branches from trees and bushes. White rhinos are larger and reside in herds of up to ten. Black rhinos live alone except for mothers and their calves, which stay together for two to three years. Rhinos have poor eyesight. They communicate with sounds and gestures, growling or snorting and curling their tails when angry.

In shallow marshes and grassy meadows, **STORKS** feed in daytime on lizards, snakes, frogs, fish, insects, and small mammals. They snap up their food with their long, pointed beaks. Storks open and close their beaks rapidly, making loud clatters. Young storks wait in their large stick nests, begging for food with croaks, whistles, and whines.

African **TERMITES** build mounds of soil, saliva, and dung to live in and for protection. The mounds can be enormous and complex, with tunnels that store nutrients and water and help keep the surrounding soil moist. Plants grow nearby and animals come to feed on them. Termites eat wood and create chambers to store it in. When they leave their mounds, snakes often move in.

Medium-sized antelope, **TOPIS** are grazers that eat only grass. They preside over large territories, called leks. The most dominant male will stay in the center of the lek, standing on a termite hill or a mound of dung to guard his territory and watch for predators.

VERVET monkeys spend most of their time in the trees. Their long arms, legs, and tail help them to climb, jump, and balance. They come down to find food but never venture far because of predators. If they sense danger, they will let out shrill screams and squeals.

Large birds of prey with a wide wingspan, **VULTURES** swoop down to feast on dead animals, called carrion. They perform an important task by helping to clean the environment and prevent the spread of diseases. Their strong immune system lets them eat rotting meat and not get sick. Sometimes they eat too much and can't fly, so they throw up to lighten their load and fly off.

WARTHOGS are wild pigs named for the bumps on their faces that resemble warts. Females live with their young in groups called "sounders." They usually search for their food at dawn and dusk. But if there's danger, they run fast back to their burrows and wait to feed under cover of night.

WILDEBEESTS, also called gnus, are members of the antelope family, though they have their own distinct look—shaggy mane, overly large head, pointed beard, and sharp curved horns for protection. They migrate over grassy plains in large herds, often alongside zebras, in search of food and water. Day and night they graze on grasses, fruits, and plants. Rather than harming grassland, they promote its growth.

ZEBRA stripes are as individual as our fingerprints. But when zebras are together in a herd, they are a puzzle of stripes, making it hard for lions or leopards to pick out one zebra to chase. Their stripes also protect against insect diseases, control body temperature, and contribute to the herd's social health.

ABOUT THE AUTHOR

KAREN B. WINNICK is the author of more than a dozen picture books for children, most of which she illustrated. An animal lover, she serves on several boards devoted to the well-being of animals. She's a graduate of Syracuse University, mother of three grown sons, grandmother of eight, and minder of five pups. She and her husband reside in Los Angeles.